If you can...

We can!

Beth Shoshan & Petra Brown

Bath · New York · Singapore · Hong Kong · Cologne · Delhi
Melbourne · Amsterdam · Johannesburg · Auckland · Shenzhen

I love you…

I really do!

(Although my arms are just too small
and so I can't quite cuddle you.)

I hug you...
    you hug me.

(And around
and around
we dance together,
holding tight.

Don't let me fall!)

I tickle you...
you giggle too.

(But not my toes...! No!
Not my toes,
you know that's when I'll squeal the most!)

I make you laugh...
you laugh with me.

(There's nothing in this world
that can make us feel so good
as laughter can, as laughter does,
as laughter should.)

I hold your hand...
you hold mine tight.

(Just feeling snug, secure, and safe.
Just knowing you'll protect me,
care for me...
be there.)

I sing you songs...
you sing them too.

(Loud ones, soft ones,
make-me-laugh ones.
Love songs, sleep songs,
safe-and-sound songs.)

I tell you tales...
you listen close.

(Then tell me stories
through the night...

of mighty dragons,
gallant knights...

adventures made
to fill my mind.)

I'm in your dreams...
and you're
in mine.

(The best dreams, safe dreams,
sleep-all-night dreams.
My dreams, your dreams.
Always our dreams.)

Let's be friends forever, I say!

There for one another,
looking out and taking care.

So…

Whatever you do...

and whatever I do…

Let's do it...

...together!

For you, me, and all of us!

B.S.

For Lewis & Samantha

P.B.

Text copyright © Beth Shoshan 2008
Illustrations copyright © Petra Brown 2008

This edition published by Parragon in 2011

Parragon
Queen Street House
4 Queen Street
Bath BA1 1HE, UK

Published by arrangement with Meadowside Children's Books
185 Fleet Street London EC4A 2HS

All rights reserved. No part of this publication may be reproduced, stored
in a retrieval system or transmitted, in any form or by any means, electronic,
mechanical, photocopying, recording or otherwise, without the prior
permission of the copyright holder.

ISBN 978-1-4454-2205-3

Printed in China